To François
To Sami
To my parents and grandparents

– Rachel Bédard

The Way to Slumbertown was first published in *Holland's Magazine* in 1916.
This Illustrated Edition © 2005 Lobster Press and David Macdonald, trustee, and Ruth Macdonald.
Illustrations © 2005 Rachel Bédard

L. M. Montgomery is a trademark of Heirs of L. M. Montgomery Inc. Used with Permission.

Published by:
Lobster Press™
1620 Sherbrooke Street West, Suites C & D
Montréal, Québec   H3H 1C9
Tel. (514) 904-1100 • Fax (514) 904-1101
www.lobsterpress.com

Publisher: Alison Fripp
Editors: Alison Fripp & Karen Li
Editorial Assistant: Stephanie Normandin
Graphic Design & Production: Tammy Desnoyers

We acknowledge the financial support of the Government of Canada through the
Book Publishing Industry Development Program (BPIDP) for our publishing activities.

We acknowledge the support of the Canada
Council for the Arts for our publishing program.

Library and Archives Canada Cataloguing in Publication

Montgomery, L. M. (Lucy Maud), 1874-1942.
        The way to Slumbertown / Lucy Maud Montgomery ; Rachel Bédard, illustrator.

ISBN 1-894222-98-9

        1. Children's poetry, Canadian (English) I. Bédard, Rachel, 1979-
II. Title.

PS8526.O55W39 2005   jC811'.52   C2005-900887-3

Printed and bound in China

The Way to Slumbertown

written by **L. M. Montgomery**

illustrated by **Rachel Bédard**

Lobster Press™

*I*f we could go to Slumbertown
within a new moon boat,

How splendid it would be
across a magic sea to float.

With silver oar and mast of pearl
and sail of old moonbeams,

Until we drop our anchor
in the Harbour of Fair Dreams.

*I*f we could fly to Slumbertown
upon a white moth's back,

What fun 'twould be to follow
on the whispering breezes' track.

*A*way above the fleecy clouds and o'er the sunset bars,

Until we lighted softly
on the Land of Evening Stars.

But after all, the surest
and the safest passage there

Is by the way of mother's arms
and mother's rocking chair.

$\mathcal{W}$e pay a kiss for fare, and then we shut our sleepy eyes

And drift before we know it
to the Coast of Lullabies.

Date Due

MAR 16 2006			